Dedicated to Ciar

Chapter 1

The road from Arklow, a small town on the east coast of Ireland, sweeps inland to Gorey before stretching on to the major seaport of Wexford. The constant flow of traffic by-passing a small isolated white-washed cottage built at the turn of the century of mud and wattling. These traditional materials are, like its inhabitants, poor, but strong enough to withstand the relentless forces of man and nature.

The cottage is perched close to the edge of a cliff, slowly submitting to the relentless pounding of a cold and inhospitable Irish sea. There are three rooms in the crumbling house. The kitchen has a large open fire, a black slate floor and a narrow wooden ladder leading to a chilly bedroom crudely built into the corrugated iron roof. The remaining room, another bedroom, is, like the rest, sparsely furnished, the poor quality of the furniture reflecting the dismal fortunes of the family it shelters.

Three people live in the cottage. Dad, Paddy, is fifty-two years old and a proud, stubborn man of over six feet with forearms as broad as a horse's hind leg. His hair is thick, wavy and as dark as a starless sky. The years have been kind to his hair, but not to his complexion, which is as craggy as the coastline he continually battles. Many years ago, he inherited the cottage from his father along with fifty acres of arable land. Today, the ruthless sea and the local bank have claimed all but four acres. High tides and interest rates have little respect for poor coastal farmers.

Mum, Nora, twenty years younger than Paddy, was born in Connemara, in a small town called Clifden. She is a slight woman with wiry red hair worn in a thick plait that hangs just below her slim waist. Her face is pale, freckled and highlighted by warm and friendly nut brown eyes. She is a gentle woman who transforms the squalid conditions of the rural cottage into a home.

Declan is aged eleven and dismayed with his stunted physique and cropped rust-coloured hair inherited from his mother. He wanted so much to be big and strong like his father Paddy. Instead, he was so small that the public health nurse found it necessary when he was 6 months old to report to

*The cottage is perched close to the edge of a cliff, slowly submitting
to the relentless pounding of a cold and inhospitable Irish sea.*

On his back he carries his school books and lunch in an old-fashioned leather satchel.

her board that Declan Brennan, in her opinion, was under-nourished. This greatly upset Mum, Nora, as she took great pride in the fact that, in the fourteen years since she had married Paddy, she had managed somehow to provide them with three nourishing meals a day.

On school days, Declan rises at six. He breakfasts on steaming hot porridge, brown bread and milky tea. With the sea thundering onto the forgotten strand below, he leaves the cottage and follows the coastline past the abandoned coast guard station to the grass track that leads to the small two-roomed schoolhouse. On his back he carries his school books and lunch in an old-fashioned leather satchel. This arduous hike through wet and muddy fields to the main Arklow road takes him almost forty minutes.

On Saturdays, Declan works for Mr O'Toole, the local landowner. He mucks out the stables and sweeps the yard. Mrs O'Toole runs a small livery yard and occasionally rewards Declan by giving him riding lessons on Sandy, a small Palomino pony. Declan is a quick learner and a natural horseman.

Chapter 2

Early one Sunday morning in March, Declan was awoken by the sound of a horse pawing on the ground directly behind the cottage. He dressed and climbed down the ladder into the kitchen. As he passed his parents' bedroom, he could clearly hear his mother tossing and turning in her bed. Declan knew that his Mum was not at all well. Last week, Dad was very worried and borrowed Mr O'Toole's old Land Rover to drive her to Loughlinstown hospital. It was the third time she had been to see Doctor McGee since Christmas.

Declan unlatched the front door and exited through the corrugated lean-to porch into the early morning mist.

It was a calm day. The sea just rolled lazily on to the sandy shore below. His hands were, as always, buried deep in his pockets. As he walked around the side of the cottage, he was startled.

Facing him was the ugliest horse he had ever

Facing him was the ugliest horse he had ever seen.

seen. The unfortunate animal had a patchy dark brown coat, stumpy cow-hocked legs and a square head with two odd coloured ears, both pointing in different directions. Her head-collar had a brass name plate with the name "Princess" clearly etched onto it.

Over the following weeks, Dad searched in vain for Princess's owners. He even placed an advertisement in 'The Wicklow People' without success.

The vet said that he was sure that Princess was at least thirty years old and probably belonged to the travellers, who abandoned her as she could neither pull a caravan nor breed foals. Sadly, he thought it unlikely that she would last another winter.

One Sunday morning at the end of May, as day broke over the isolated cottage, Declan was awoken by the sound of Princess moving about outside. He dressed quickly and made his way down the rickety stairs. He noticed that his parents' bedroom door was ajar. He could hear his Mum, who had been confined to bed for the last two weeks moaning softly while his Dad recited the rosary.

Confused, Declan went outside to look for Princess. At first, he ran along the cliff edge, then he followed the steps carved into the stalwart rocks all the way down to beach. There was no sign of the raggedy horse anywhere.

He decided to go back to the cottage. As he reached the front door, he came upon his father framed in the doorway. Tears were streaming down his ruddy cheeks.

"Declan, your Mother has passed away," he said. "Her suffering is over. God has finally released her from the miserable life of poverty and pain I subjected her to. Before she died, she asked me to tell you that she loved you and to remember that this parting is only temporary."

Declan could not conceive that his mother was dead and that he would never again bury his head in her wondrous flowing curls.

That afternoon the undertaker arrived and laid his mother out in her favourite floral summer dress. Declan thought that she looked far too beautiful to be dead. He watched over her, convinced that at any moment she would wake up and this nightmare would be over until, that is, he kissed the reality of her cold, lifeless lips.

When old Father Murphy arrived that afternoon, Declan took a lead rope and went out again to look for Princess. It was a pleasant day

*He found Princess lying underneath the majestic oak tree
close to the old fairy fort.*

and Declan climbed the steep stony path towards the headland. To his delight, he found Princess lying in the sun underneath the majestic oak tree close to the old fairy fort. He called out her name and ran over to where she lay.

Princess was motionless. Beside her, to his surprise, stood a filly foal no more than a few hours old. Declan fell to his knees. Something was wrong with Princess. She was not breathing.

Declan did everything he could to revive Princess, but he was too late. She had, he reasoned, died giving birth to the foal.

Declan jumped to his uncertain feet and left the foal curled up by its dead mother in the shade of the oak tree. He ran all the way back to the cottage. He found Dad and Father Murphy talking to Ned, an old fashioned journeyman with long grey hair and a beard that sat in a wiry bush on his broad chest. Ned, despite his dishevelled appearance, was of noble birth and chose to travel the country on an old black bicycle doing odd jobs. He was a learned man who often called to poor people in times of hardship to offer sympathy and advice. His payment was a tot of whiskey, a hot meal and a roof over his head for the night.

Breathless with excitement, Declan relayed his

story. Old Ned looked anxious and asked Declan to describe Princess, then requested that he be brought immediately to see her and the foal. Declan ran ahead with Dad while Father Murphy and Ned followed close behind.

When they reached the oak tree, the foal was standing obediently where Declan had left him, but there was no sign of Princess. Paddy's rage broke the silence.

"Declan, tell the truth in front of the Holy Father. What have you done with the mare and where did you steal this filly foal from? I cannot believe that you would do such a thing with your poor mother laid out below in the house and not dead five hours yet. Father, you may rest assured the child will be severely punished!!!"

Ned, who had been kneeling, stood and pointed to the ground beneath the oak tree.

"The child does not lie, Paddy. Look, a horse lay here within the hour. The ground is warm and has been disturbed by the unfortunate animal being dragged towards the cliff face."

Old Ned walked over to the edge of the cliff and pointed to the sea below. On the rocks framed by the rising tide, her head cradled on a mound of soft sea weed, was Princess.

*When they reached the oak tree, the foal stood obediently
where Declan had left him*

Declan, bewildered and deeply upset, was instructed to return to the cottage alone. Paddy and Father Murphy followed an hour later with Ned leading the excitable foal.

Declan warmed some milk and hand fed the hungry foal. While he was doing this, Ned spoke to Paddy.

"Princess is a fairy horse with special powers! She belongs to no man. She is a free spirit that has roamed the seashores of Ireland for over one thousand years. She is the seventh consecutive filly foal from the same dam. The owners of the land she grazes are protected from other world beings and forces invisible to the human eye. By day she will be of this world, but as night falls she will return to the sea that nurtures her, to graze on the lush sea grass. This day the water fairies and the sea have reclaimed Princess and, in return, have left this sprightly pony foal in your care. Paddy, love, cherish and protect this foal and, believe me, you will be well rewarded."

Chapter 3

Ned, it turned out, spoke wisely because from that day on the family's fortunes changed miraculously. The morning after Nora's funeral, Mr O'Toole called to the cottage. His farm manager was retiring and he offered Paddy the job.

Paddy worked very hard over the following months and was well rewarded by Mr O'Toole. He soon had enough money put aside to refurbish and even extend the old cottage. A bedroom for Declan, a bathroom and a small stable for the foal were soon added.

On Christmas day Paddy and Declan joined the O'Tooles for dinner. Mr O'Toole surprised Paddy by presenting him with the old Land Rover.

Their first family excursion in the Land Rover was to the cinema in Arklow to see *Batman*. After the film, Paddy brought Declan to the Yankee Doodle restaurant for his first American-style burger and an extra thick chocolate milkshake.

The following two years passed very quickly. The basics of life were quickly augmented with the luxuries: a television, washing machine and a dishwasher. All this time, the Connemara foal, who had been named "Titania" after the Fairy Queen, observed the changing fortunes from her small paddock overlooking the cottage.

On the third anniversary of his mothers death, Declan began breaking Titania. Mrs O'Toole helped willingly. Titania had developed into a beautifully proportioned pony, a prime example of her proud Connemara breed. She was steel grey in colour with a contrasting white mane and tail.

Declan would talk to Titania for hours at night before going to bed. He thought she looked almost human. He once admitted to his Dad that he was certain that she had the same dark nut brown eyes as his mother.

It was obvious from the very first day that Titania was taken into Mrs. O'Toole's sand arena that she was special. It was almost as if she had done it all before. Within days, Declan and the spirited Titania were galloping fearlessly along the seashore, across the fields, effortlessly clearing ditches, dikes and gates.

During the summer, Titania and Declan were

They won all their showing and jumping classes in every gymkhana, horse and agricultural show from Waterford to Dublin.

the most celebrated junior show jumping combination on the east coast.

They won all their showing and jumping classes in every horse and agricultural show from Waterford to Dublin. The bond between them was uncanny. Declan and Titania were, it seemed, as one.

At the end of September, the show jumping season came to an end and Titania was put out to grass for a well-earned rest.

Chapter 4

One Sunday night in late October, as the swirling rain and biting wind beat against the walls of the cottage, Declan awoke with a start. He thought he heard the sound of a lorry moving through one of Mr O'Toole's fields. He looked at his watch and wondered what on earth anyone would be doing close to midnight on such a night like this. No good, he thought.

Headlights reflected on the ceiling of his bedroom.

Declan jumped out of bed to investigate further. His father Paddy was already standing by the kitchen window, looking out in to the darkness.

"Get dressed son, and run directly to Mr O'Toole's farm. Inform him that there are men in the top paddock … Run quickly."

Declan put his wax mack and boots on over his pyjamas and ran to inform Mr O'Toole.

When Declan and Mr O'Toole reached the gate

leading into the top paddock, they could see and hear the horses that had earlier been grazing contentedly now galloping excitedly around the field.

Declan and Mr O'Toole ran across the field to Paddy. They found him standing silently staring in the direction of the fading lights of the lorry.

"I'm sorry, son. I could not stop them. It was Titania they were after."

The following morning, Declan was already in the kitchen when the buzzer on his alarm clock announced it was time to get up for school.

This morning, of all mornings, he did not have to be told. He was already washed, dressed and making his way out the door - not to school, but to the Garda Station in Arklow.

The Gardai had no word for Declan. It seemed that Titania had simply disappeared into thin air. Regardless, Declan sat in the cold waiting room, his duffel coat pulled up around his ears, waiting for word.

When the Sergeant returned from lunch and saw Declan shivering pitifully in the corner, he immediately called for a squad car to take him home. Declan went reluctantly.

At home in the warm kitchen, he relaxed in a

comfortable chair and stared blankly into the open fire.

Soon he was asleep and dreaming of the oak tree close to the fairy fort. He could feel warm sunlight on his back and smell fresh flowers. A sense of total well-being, which he had never experienced before, washed over him.

He thought he heard a noise on the other side of the oak tree and went to investigate.

Seated before him, a hammer in one hand, mending a pair of tiny shoes, was the strangest man he had ever seen.

He was ugly and of stunted growth with a face like dried apples. Yet his eyes were mischievous and bright. He wore a long grey coat over a bright red jacket and breeches buckled at the knee. Around his neck was an Elizabethan ruff and lace frills at his wrist. His stockings were grey to match his top coat. Over his knees, to protect his clothes, he draped a leather apron. On the ground beside him was a red cocked hat.

Chapter 5

"If those darned fairies didn't dance so much, they wouldn't wear out their shoes so quickly," the little man declared angrily, pointing to the pile of shoes on the ground next to him. He continued impatiently.

"You must be Declan. I was told to expect you. My name is Ronan. In my world, I am a solitary fairy. In yours, I am known as a Fear Dearg. I have been requested by Áine, Queen of the trooping fairies, to link our worlds so that Titania may be rescued from the evil men who stole her. In order that we may do this, you must first cross over to our world. Do you wish to enter the fairy kingdom and rescue Titania ?"

Declan was quite taken aback by the arrogant, unfriendly tone of the Fear Dearg. It was as if he were reluctantly carrying out this request for the fairies.

"Yes, of course. I would do anything to save

"First of all, we both must eat a magic oak seed."

Titania. Just direct me," replied Declan hopefully.

"First of all, we both must eat a magic oak seed," Ronan said, taking two from a small leather pouch tied at his waist. He handed Declan one of the dried seeds and selected another for himself.

"They will shrink us to the size of a pin head, thus making us invisible to mortals and allowing us enter the fairy world."

Declan placed the seed on his tongue and swallowed. At first, nothing happened. Then, all of a sudden, he had this strange sensation of his legs folding and the ground racing up to meet him. Declan stumbled and fell on his back. When he stood and dusted himself down, he realised that he was the same size as Ronan.

The oak tree now towered for miles into the sky. The trunk was like a mountain and the tiny pebbles that lay around the loamy base were now huge boulders.

Ronan clapped his hands and from high above two enormous, almost transparent wings began to flap and descend towards them. The noise and the down-draught created by the huge wingspan as it neared the ground almost knocked Declan over. When the animal landed, Declan realised that it was a magnificent butterfly. Its delicate wings shimmered yellow and were edged in pearls and diamonds.

Ronan climbed awkwardly along the butterfly's wing and settled in the warm hairs at the back of its head. Declan followed tentatively. Ronan instructed him to hold on tight. Without warning, the butterfly leapt into the air and began to fly up towards the sturdy branches of the noble oak tree.

As they passed over the lowest of the branches, Declan looked down and rubbed his eyes in disbelief. Below, stretching into the distant horizon, were large fields of corn, wheat, barley and rolling green pasture, grazed contentedly by cows, sheep and horses. Parallel were smaller fields of fruit trees and vegetables.

Everywhere, tending the crops, were similarly dressed fairies in red leather boots, blue denim dungarees and white collarless shirts.

These fairies did not have the same facial features as Ronan. In fact, they looked more like ants. Ronan, noticing Declan's confusion, explained.

"They are Worker Fairies. Their function is to tend the crops and provide food and fodder for the Harvest Fairies. You see, there are no seasons in our world. That is how we can grow summer crops all year round."

"They are Worker Fairies. Their function is to tend the crops and provide food and fodder for the Harvest Fairies."

The delicate butterfly climbed higher and higher, expertly negotiating the intricate pattern of branches. Ronan explained to Declan, as they glided towards the fairy palace,

"The oak tree shelters a complex fairy world, unseen by mortals. On every level or branch there is a colony. The first is the farming colony. Their duties are to provide food for the tables. The second is the industrial level where the grain is milled, the wool spun and the dairy produce separated into milk, cream, cheese and butter. Honey and nuts donated by the bees and squirrels are stored here in huge warehouses.

The third level is where the artisan or Worker Fairies live. Their houses are carved from the branches by the Wood Fairies. Those considered to be the Skilled Fairies live on the next level, just below the entrance to the Palace."

"What is your job?" Declan enquired, inquisitively.

Ronan looked at Declan impatiently and replied,

"I am described by your world as a Fear Dearg. In the fairy world, I am a simple cobbler. I make and repair brogues, sandals and slippers for the entire fairy tribe living here in the branches of the oak tree. It is a tiresome and time-consuming job as the fairies continually wear out their shoes dancing."

As he spoke, Ronan lit up his dudeen, a foul smelling stump of a pipe. Fear Deargs, or solitary fairies are by nature dour and ill-mannered, tolerated by the mild-mannered fairies only because of their skills in shoe-making and their ability to guard their fairy treasure against mortals.

The large gates of the Fairy Palace loomed ahead. The butterfly hovered for a moment on a current of warm air as the hand-carved doors creaked open to reveal an enormous corridor lined in thin sheets of shimmering red gold and lit by thousands of tulip shaped glass crystal lamps.

The butterfly landed gently. Declan followed Ronan down its silken wings and jumped to the ground, gravelled in millions of sparkling cut-diamonds. While Declan gazed in wonderment, two grey horses pulling a glass chariot arrived to take Declan and Ronan to the Fairy Palace. The two fine horses, driven by a tiny fairy man, galloped tirelessly over the gravelled diamonds to the Palace.

Declan and Ronan were met and shown into the Palace by six military fairies. These powerful-

*Inside the enormous chamber were hundreds of beautiful, blond,
blue-eyed fairies singing and dancing.*

*Declan was awe-struck. He had never seen anyone
or anything so beautiful.*

looking men were dressed in brown leather knee boots and waistcoats worn over white shirts and red breeches.

They were marched along an endless array of finely decorated corridors to the fairy Áine's private chamber.

Inside the enormous room were hundreds of beautiful, blond, blue-eyed fairies singing and dancing, their pale, layered, chiffon dresses studded in minute diamonds and red rubies. The chamber was wondrous. The floor was covered in red, yellow and white rose petals, the walls in delicately patterned white marble and the ceiling sparkled with glass crystal droplets.

From over Declan's shoulder a fanfare of trumpets heralded the arrival of the Fairy Queen, Áine, with her entourage of maidservants. The chamber fell silent as she glided to her throne, carved from bog oak which was over ten thousand years old. Declan was awe-struck. He had never seen anyone or anything so beautiful.

Áine stood proud and erect before her golden throne and subjects. Her long blond hair, which fell loosely to her waist, was intertwined with fresh flower blossoms. Her eyes were as clear and blue as a summer sky, and her skin as smooth and delicate as a buttercup. Her dress was of the finest white silk and shimmered as she spoke. Her voice was as soft as a kitten purring.

"Declan, you are indeed welcome to the unseen world. My name is the fairy Áine. Firstly, you must understand that the good fortune you have enjoyed since your dear mother's death was not by chance, but decreed here by the Fairy Council. We were aware that your mother, Nora, was unwell and summoned her to a better life among the stars. In return, we left Titania. Ronan, your appointed guardian, now reports that some evil men have stolen Titania.

Áine beckoned Declan closer to the throne and spoke directly to him.

"We have little time. If the evil men who stole Titania attempt to escape by sea, a terrible disaster will befall not only them, but all that travel aboard the ship. Princess and Titania are water-fairies from a magical land deep below the sea. They were born of that land and will ultimately return to it. The sea will claim her own and if others are to be sacrificed in this act then, unfortunately, so be it. Be mindful that fairy magic only works on Irish mortals and should Titania be sold to men from other nations, our magic is useless."

Áine clapped her hands and called for the fairy man in charge of the aviary. In the blink of an eye, a fairy with the body of a man and the head of an eagle appeared.

"I want you to summon all the robins," Áine instructed the aviary fairy. "Inform them that the seventh filly of the seventh dam has been stolen. They are to fly to the four corners of this land and not rest until Titania has been found. You must also instruct our friends the sea gulls to watch over all the sea ports. We have no time to waste. Ronan, take Declan to your house and offer him some fairy hospitality. I will send for you when we have word on Titania."

Chapter 6

Declan followed Ronan as he stomped indignantly down the winding golden staircase to the lower level where the irritable Fear Dearg lived. While the elite fairies lived within the confines and splendour of the palace, the artisan fairies lived in modest single-room houses, delicately carved from the branches of the oak tree. Paths, roadways and canals to carry water had been chiselled out of the bark. All the rainwater was collected and distributed to the homes, factories and farms. In summer months, when the rainfall was poor, starlings would fetch and carry water for the fairies.

Ronan brought Declan into his house, which was filled with a wide variety of shoes, sandals and slippers. Declan sat down to rest at the kitchen table. Everything in the house was highly polished and expertly carved out of wood. Ronan ignored Declan and began repairing a pair of pixie boots.

Ronan mumbled angrily all the way back to the Palace.

After an hour of enforced silence, and in an attempt to make conversation, Declan enquired where fairies came from. Ronan begrudgingly replied.

"When God created the world, he accepted that there would undoubtedly be two forces: one good, the other evil. He was, of course, mindful that if the balance should swing in the wrong direction that the earth could destroy itself. His solution was simple. He created fairies as his representatives on earth to watch over and adjust the balance. When he accomplished his task, he placed the fairies on a cloud of stardust and dispatched them to earth."

Ronan was interrupted by a knock on the door.

"Who is bothering me now?" he called out.

"You are ordered by the Fairy Queen Áine to return to the Palace immediately," a gentle voice replied.

Ronan mumbled angrily all the way back to the Palace.

When they arrived, the fairy Áine was waiting for them at the door to her chambers.

"I have received a report from a robin in Laois that Titania has been spotted in an outhouse at the back of an old farm near the village of Timahoe. The house belongs to an elderly horse dealer known to us as Mad Jack. Word is that she is to be auctioned at the horse and pony sales in Goresbridge, County Kilkenny Saturday next."

"I will inform the Gardai immediately," Declan exclaimed gleefully.

"You will do no such thing," declared Áine. "Titania, like Princess, is a free spirit destined to roam this land for ten more generations. She belongs to no mortal. It is almost dark now, Declan. You must return to your world. Next Saturday morning at day break, report to Ronan at the base of the oak tree and be mindful to dress warmly. Mr O'Toole will not require you to work in the yard that day as he and your father are travelling to Slane to inspect a herd of Charolais cattle. Remember Declan, do not tell anyone of this adventure. If you do, the spell will be broken and Titania will be lost forever."

With that she handed Declan a dried oak seed, which he swallowed, then clapped her hands. Declan awoke back in the cottage, seated in the old fireside chair.

Chapter 7

Declan did not believe in fairies and was certain that this meeting with the fairy Áine had only been a dream.

Late on Friday night, however, when Paddy announced that Mr O'Toole and himself were indeed travelling to Slane on Saturday and that he would be required to work Sunday instead of Saturday, Declan knew for certain that he had somehow travelled to the unseen world.

He woke at day break. Paddy had already left for Slane. He dressed warmly as the fairy Áine had advised and devoured a bowl of steaming porridge before sprinting up the cliff path to the oak tree.

He found Ronan mending a pair of worn ballet slippers. The fastening ribbon was frayed and torn. He had to cut and hand-stitch a new piece of ribbon. Ronan ignored Declan until he had finished mending the slipper then, without uttering a word, handed Declan an oak seed. Together they entered the unseen world. After a few minutes silence, the sky darkened and a large grey sparrow hawk appeared in the sky and landed close by.

Declan, unprepared for the hawk, was sent tumbling head over heels with the down draught created by the bird's enormous wings. When he managed to get back to his feet, Ronan appeared from behind the safety of a large boulder. Declan was annoyed with Ronan, but decided it was more important to find Titania than argue with the horrible little man.

As they mounted the sturdy wing-feathers of the hawk, Ronan informed Declan that they would be travelling with the majestic bird on the longest part of the journey to Borris in County Carlow. There they would be met by the robin who found Titania in Timahoe. She would take them on to the Goresbridge sales yard, which was quite close by.

The hawk flexed its enormous muscles and propelled itself skywards. At first he flew effortlessly out to sea, then he climbed higher before doubling back, passing over the cottage and the foaming waves breaking on the shore. The sea gulls squawked nervously and scattered in every direction as this efficient hunter passed menacingly overhead. The hawk followed the coastline to

The sky darkened and a large grey sparrow hawk appeared.

Courtown, then moved inland, passing over Gorey and Ferns. As Mount Leinster approached, the hawk climbed higher and the air became noticeably colder.

They reached Borris just after eight o'clock. They were early. The robin had not arrived yet. The hawk landed as arranged on a large estate just outside the village.

They did not have long to wait for the robin. It was obvious by her nervous disposition when she arrived that she, like all the other birds, had the highest of respect for the powerful sparrow hawk.

Declan and Ronan clambered down from their lofty perch and transferred to the less distinguished robin.

Chapter 8

When they arrived in Goresbridge, the robin landed on the corner of a stable overlooking one of the outdoor sand arenas. It was here that prospective buyers observed the horses and ponies being put through their paces prior to entering the sales ring.

There was a motley assortment of well-groomed ponies, each of their eager owners vying to catch the attention of the big cross-channel dealers. One, however, stood proud: number twelve, a grey Connemara pony called Titania.

Declan cried. He was not sure if it was from relief or fear.

The whole complex from the main street to the car park at the rear was filled to capacity with lorries and horse boxes. The sand arenas were teeming, not only with horses and ponies, but men, women, children, vets, stewards and dealers — every one of them an expert, awarding critical or appreciative nods to each bewildered animal as it passed. The sales catalogue, their bible, was rolled into a tube and freely smacked off Land Rovers, stable doors and the behinds of startled horses and ponies.

Over in one sand arena, a chubby boy Declan's age was riding Titania. He was Mad Jack's son Henry! He was waiting his turn to jump a practice fence. He was encountering great difficulty controlling Titania, who was prancing and snorting. When Henry's turn came to jump, Mad Jack waddled over to the jump and raised the poles five holes, leaving the sturdy fence at close to six feet high. There was an air of expectancy around the arena as the boy circled Titania one more time and turned towards the fence. The little Connemara pony galloped confidently into the imposing jump. She was undaunted by the height, having cleared higher obstacles in the past. As she tensed her muscles to leap over the jump and the unsuspecting boy duly leaned forward assuming the correct jumping position, Titania dug her hooves in and stopped. The boy, however, did not and sailed over the brightly coloured poles. He landed in a crumpled heap on the other side of the fence, his head buried in the gritty sand.

While the disgruntled Henry dusted the sand from his clothes and out of his ears, Mad Jack scowled and walked across the arena to retrieve the erring Titania.

Declan, despite his heartbreak, applauded. But not for long as Henry now ran towards Titania with his whip raised over his head. When he reached the defenceless pony, he brought the whip down savagely between its ears. The laughter that a few moments ago had greeted the boy's demise now turned to disgust.

Unperturbed, the boy remounted Titania and, with the poles replaced, once again turned her into the fence. There was a tremendous air of expectancy as Titania approached the jump. This time, three strides out, the boy in anticipation passed the reins into his left hand, raised his crop and dug his spurs deep into Titania's side. Titania sailed effortlessly over the jump, displaying a grace and poise rarely witnessed in Gorsebridge. The dealers turned away well satisfied.

Mad Jack led Titania triumphantly from the arena. Ronan informed Declan that they would have to move quickly now as it would not be long before the auction began. As Titania was number twelve, she would be one of the first into the ring.

The robin followed Mad Jack to where Titania

*He landed in a crumpled heap on the other side of the fence,
his head buried in the soft sand.*

was stabled, a bare concrete structure overlooking the lorry park. She landed on the corrugated roof over the stable. After a short while, Mad Jack came out of the stable and began talking to a dealer. Ronan removed an odd-looking hawthorn stick from his pocket and pointed it at the clear blue sky and said:

Cloudless sky devoid of pain,
Cleanse our souls and bring us rain.

Mad Jack sat down to rest on an old garden bench. He soon fell asleep. Behind him on the distant horizon dark rain clouds suddenly appeared.

Ronan instructed the robin to fly over and hover above Mad Jack's shoulder. The robin obeyed. When they were in position, Ronan called on Declan, who reluctantly followed him, diving headlong into the soft wool of Mad Jack's tweed jacket.

"Come on, follow me. There is no time to waste," shouted Ronan.

They ran across the shoulder of Mad Jack's jacket, which was quite difficult as the weave of the tweed was very wide. When they reached the revere, they slid down the underside and ended up close to a large leather button. Ronan now moved inside the jacket. Declan followed. They climbed down until they were opposite the waistband of Mad Jack's brown cord trousers.

"This is the easy bit," shouted Ronan. "Close your eyes and jump!"

Ronan hurled himself into the centre of the wide channels of Mad Jack's cord trousers and slid down at great speed into the turn-ups. Declan was not so sure but, nevertheless, closed his eyes and jumped, never daring to open them all the way down.

With some difficulty, they climbed out of the turn-up, jumped down onto Mad Jack's socks and squeezed through a small opening in his tooled leather brogues. By the time Declan caught up with Ronan, he had already begun filing away at the sole of one of Mad Jack's shoes. In a couple more minutes, he had expertly cut a hole the size of a one pound coin in the sole of the shoe.

Ronan, pleased with his workmanship, gathered up his tools and eased his way up the inside of the shoe, exiting through a small gap left between the lace and an eyelet. Declan followed. He was not as agile as the Fear Dearg and was clearly tired.

Ronan, aware of Declan's difficulties, smiled. When they emerged into the bright sunlight, Mad

An enormous black spider scuttled along the beam towards the robin.

Jack was still sleeping. They jumped to the ground and ran across the path to Titania's stable door, avoiding giant hooves, feet and stones on the way.

The robin, seeing them, swooped down and carried the two adventurers back to the safety of their lofty perch on top of the stable block.

"Now," Ronan said to the robin. "We have more work to do. You must take us to the shop of the local shoemaker at the other end of the village."

The robin flapped his small wings and flew out over the rooftops of the sales ring and houses, landing on a telephone pole opposite the shoemaker's. The small shop was open. The robin flew in the door and perched high in the rafters. The old shoemaker was seated close to a coal fire reading the Irish Independent. An enormous black spider scuttled along the beam towards the robin. Ronan climbed down from the robin and spoke sternly to the hairy spider.

"Spin me a web this instance or I shall bury you deep in the bowels of the earth."

Ronan climbed up onto the back of the spider and took firm hold of a large tuft of hair. The ugly spider spun a delicate web leading down to a neat pile of leather shoe soles on the counter. Without dismounting from the spider's back, Ronan once again removed the magical blackthorn stick from his pocket and pointed it at a leather sole on the top of the pile.

The spider stood obediently while Ronan placed his curse, then returned him safely to the rafters.

"My work is almost done," Ronan declared proudly. "Robin, take us to a sheltered position overlooking the entrance to the sales ring so we might observe our prey."

Declan was confused and unable to unravel the fiendish plan Ronan had devised to rescue Titania.

Chapter 9

Declan's heart began to pound, when Mad Jack's son, Henry, appeared from the stable-block leading Titania towards the sales ring. The auction was about to start.

Suddenly, the sky went dark and it began to rain. Declan had never seen anything like it. The rain came down in sheets and the noise as it beat on the old corrugated roof was deafening.

Not far behind Titania was Mad Jack. He was puffing and panting, trying to get in out of the downpour. As he ran across to the sales ring, he stepped in a puddle that had gathered on the wet, sandy ground. He stopped and removed the shoe in which Ronan had earlier cut a hole. He shook his head in disbelief and ran over to speak to his son, Henry, who was standing ever closer to the sales ring.

Mad Jack looked at his watch, ran out the gate and up the road towards the shoemaker's.

"Put a new sole on this shoe," Mad Jack demanded as he tossed his damaged shoe on the counter. "And in double quick time, too. I have a pony entering the sales ring across the road in five minutes and I must not be late."

The shoemaker picked up the leather sole Ronan had earlier placed the spell on.

The robin flew into an empty stable.

"Now, Declan, it is your turn," Ronan said. "You must take this oak seed and return to your mortal size. Approach young Henry and inform him that Mad Jack is in the shoemaker's, but left his wallet in the lorry and cannot pay. Henry must fetch the wallet immediately and bring it to him. Henry will leave Titania with you while he carries out this errand. When he is out of sight, you must grasp the opportunity and gallop Titania to the old church ruins on the horizon and wait for us there.

Declan swallowed the oak seed and returned to his mortal size, then set about following Ronan's instructions.

He left the stable and ran across the yard towards Titania. He was so excited. When Titania saw Declan, she swung around and pranced for joy. Declan quickly relayed his story to Henry. Just as Ronan had predicted, the boy handed

*He stopped and removed the shoe in which Ronan
had earlier cut a hole.*

Titania never hesitated, clearing stone walls, ditches, hedges and drains while galloping on to the old ruins.

Titania's lead rope to Declan.

Declan cried for joy as he embraced Titania, but was mindful that they must make their escape immediately. When Henry turned the corner into the lorry park, Declan mounted Titania and faced her towards the old ruins. The willing pony never hesitated as she galloped to the horizon, clearing stone walls, ditches, hedges and drains. Declan could hardly hold on, even though he clutched a fistful of Titania's flowing white mane.

They did not have too long to wait for Ronan. The robin landed on the top of a stone wall just above Declan's shoulder. There was a tiny puff of smoke and Ronan appeared before them. He was smiling. This was the first time Declan had seen the cranky Fear Dearg display any friendly emotion.

"Well done, everybody. But we must make haste from here and return to Arklow before dark. Declan, there is no need for you to return to the unseen world. You can confidently gallop Titania home from here. She is faster than the wind itself. You will be seated by a blazing fire in good time for your father's return. I bid you farewell and good fortune."

Declan shook Ronan's bony hand warmly and

thanked him for all his help. He wondered, of course, what happened to Mad Jack. His question was about to be answered.

From the road below he could hear angry voices. Declan looked quizzically at Ronan as they crouched down out of sight behind a hedge. Within a couple of minutes, Mad Jack passed. He was walking at a furious pace, his face red and fit to explode. He was roaring at his son Henry, jogging behind him.

"What have you done to Mad Jack?" whispered Declan.

"I put a fairy spell on the sole of his shoe. Mad Jack will no longer cause unhappiness. His destiny is to walk the highways and byways of this land forevermore."

Ronan whistled and the robin flew over and perched on the wall beside him. The jubilant Fear Dearg took a magic oak seed from his pocket, shook Declan's hand again and swallowed the seed. As he disappeared, the robin flew from the church wall and landed on the ground close to where Ronan had stood moments earlier. After a short while, the red-breasted bird flapped his wings, circled Declan once and flew off towards Borris.

Declan relaxed and allowed Titania to graze

awhile on the lush green grass before they too set off on their journey home.

Chapter 10

Declan was delighted to have been reunited with Titania. He stroked her long white mane lovingly as she munched the sweet grass close to the ruins.

Declan was also impatient to return home, but was mindful that it could be difficult holding onto Titania crossing Mount Leinster. So he made a sturdy neck-strap of rope in order that he may be more secure on her back.

Declan and Titania soon set off across the fields, covering the maximum of ground in the minimum of time. The speedy steel grey pony careered wildly, passing houses, startled farmers and farm animals.

In fact as they came out of Borris, Titania, while galloping along the headland, even passed a speeding car on a road running parallel to the field.

Declan closed his eyes and held on firmly to the thick rope around Titania's neck. He was almost blown backwards off Titania by the force of the wind she was creating as they cut through the thin mountain air of Mount Leinster. Declan's hands and fingers were numbed by the cold. The journey from Borris to Arklow was almost forty miles, but Declan had faith in Titania's ability and stamina. In fact, it seemed that the longer Titania galloped, the stronger she appeared to grow.

When they reached the bank of the river Slaney, Titania, without hesitation, dived into the freezing water and swam boldly and confidently across to the opposite bank.

The game little pony galloped effortlessly and skilfully across fields and roads, clearing ditches, hedges and drains until she reached her stable door overlooking the seashore in Arklow.

Declan led Titania into her warm stable and set about making her a bran mash.

It was almost dark now. Dad and Mr O'Toole had not yet returned from Slane.

During the journey home, Declan had pondered how he would explain to his Dad where Titania had suddenly appeared from. He decided that the best and easiest thing to do was to return to the oak tree and seek guidance from the fairy Áine.

With Titania watered and fed, Declan ran up to

the oak tree. When he arrived, he was totally unprepared for what he found. The once splendid oak tree was in ashes. Only a small piece of the trunk remained. The branches, where fields of corn, wheat and barley had once grown, were now smouldering on the ground where they fell.

What on earth happened to the oak tree and its fairy colony in Declan's absence?

The once splendid oak tree was in ashes.